REGULAR

GUIDE TO LIFE

BY TRACEY WEST

PSS!
Price Stern Sloan
An Imprint of Penguin Group (USA) LLC

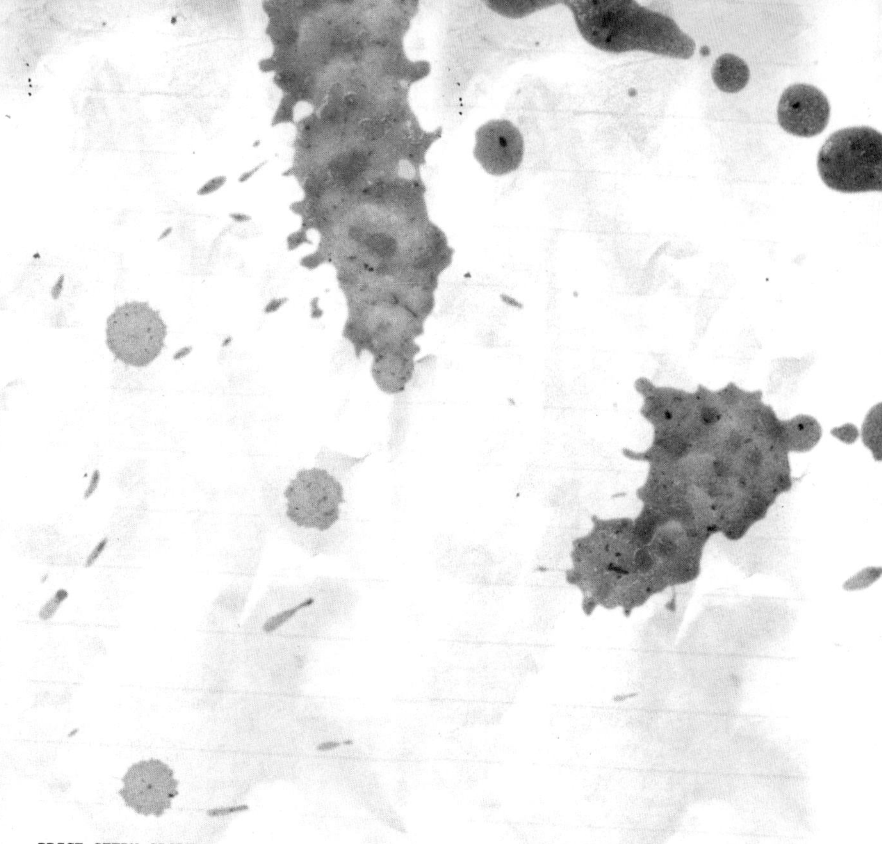

PRICE STERN SLOAN
Published by the Penguin Group
Penguin Group (USA) LLC, 375 Hudson Street, New York, New York 10014, USA

USA | Canada | UK | Ireland | Australia | New Zealand | India | South Africa | China

penguin.com
A Penguin Random House Company

Published in 2014 by Price Stern Sloan, a division of Penguin Young Readers Group, 345 Hudson Street, New York, New York 10014. *PSS!* is a registered trademark of Penguin Group (USA) LLC. Printed in the USA.

ISBN 978-0-8431-8088-6

10 9 8 7 6 5 4 3 2 1

WELCOME FROM SAM MARIN, VOICE OF MUSCLE MAN

A word of caution to the reader . . .

This book is not intended for individuals who are not ready to live life on the edge.

If you have a problem with consuming large amounts of chicken wings, waving your shirt in the air in public, or spending a day lifting nonstop at the gym, then I suggest you put this book down and read no further. If you are prepared for your life to be completely hard-core, then turn the page . . . Woo-hoooooooo!!!

—Sam,
aka Muscle Man

MEET MUSCLE MAN

Name:	Muscle Man
Full Name:	Mitch Huge Sorrenstein
Best Friend:	Hi-Five Ghost
Girlfriend:	Starla
Likes:	Rocking out, spinning doughnuts in a golf cart, eating, wrecking cars in the crash pit
Dislikes:	Losers, fancy people
Quote:	"Oh no, bro!"

CHAPTER ONE
BEING MUSCLE MAN IS
AWESOME
WHO HAS A MORE AWESOME LIFE THAN ME?
NO ONE, BRO!
I'VE GOT EVERYTHING A GUY COULD WANT.
A SWEET JOB, A GREAT BEST FRIEND,
A ROCKING BODY, A PLACE TO LIVE,
AND A LADY TO LOVE.
IT CAN'T GET ANY MORE AWESOME THAN THAT!

A DAY IN THE LIFE OF MUSCLE MAN

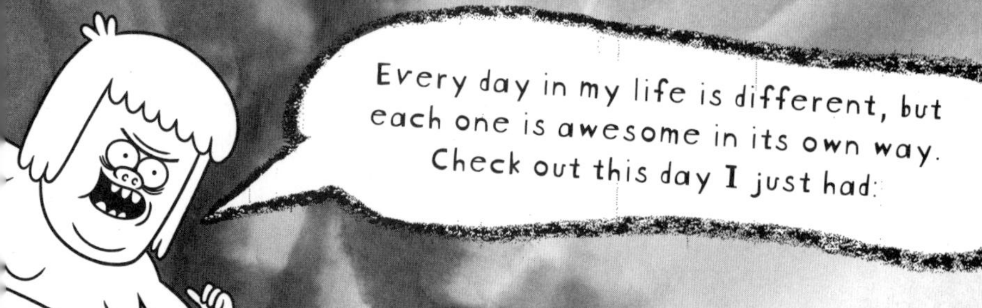

8:45 A.M.: Woke up from a sweet dream. I was performing a drum solo at a Barracuda Deathwish concert, and I rocked so hard the drums exploded.

8:50 A.M.: Tripped over a pizza box on the floor. There was a slice inside. Woo-hoo! Free breakfast!

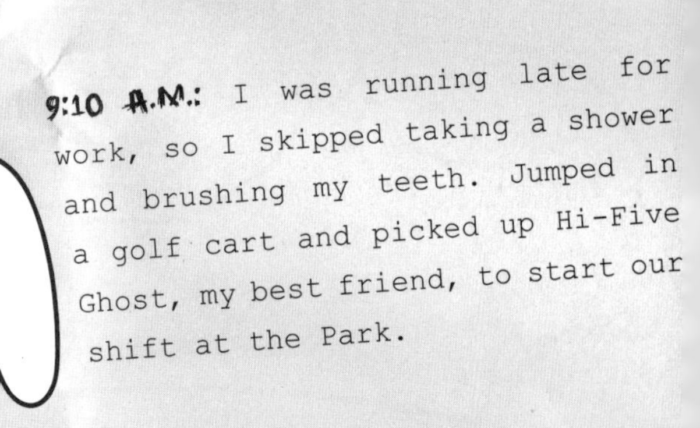

9:10 A.M.: I was running late for work, so I skipped taking a shower and brushing my teeth. Jumped in a golf cart and picked up Hi-Five Ghost, my best friend, to start our shift at the Park.

9:20 A.M.: Benson didn't notice we were late because he was yelling at Mordecai and Rigby about something. Fives and I headed over to the bandstand to mow the lawn. The weather was pretty sweet, so we took a break to catch some rays.

12:00 P.M.: Lunchtime! I was craving some spicy meat, so my friend Jimmy at the Taco'Clock food truck hooked up Fives and me.

1:00 P.M.: After downing a dozen tacos, a siesta was required, bro.

1:30 P.M.: A loud explosion woke up Fives and me. This robot dragon was totally destroying the Park. I grabbed my jumper cables and short-circuited that sucker. Woo-hoo! Took my shirt off and did some victory doughnuts in the golf cart to celebrate.

1:45 P.M.: Turns out Mordecai and Rigby summoned the dragon out of some cursed video game or something, so Benson made them clean up the Park. Afternoon off for Fives and me!

2:00 P.M.: Played some basketball with Fives. He always wins because he's great at dunking.

3:30 P.M.: My turn on the house computer. I could watch that *Mega-Wedgie* video a million times.

4:30 P.M.: Played a game of chess with Pops. What? You didn't think I knew how?

6:30 P.M.: Got ready for my date. Put on a new blue shirt. Found it under the bed.

7:00 P.M.: Dinner with my lady, Starla, at our favorite place, Wing Kingdom. She looks beautiful when she gets barbecue sauce on her chin.

8:30: P.M.: Starla and I took a romantic walk under the stars. Hey, bros, look, I had to take one for the team. If my lady ain't happy, nobody's happy.

10:00 P.M.: Back home. Watched *Cease and Deceased* for the fortieth time. It never gets old.

12:00 A.M.: Time for some late-night pie. Some stupid stress machine told me to lay off it, but no way am I giving up my late-night pie.

1:00 A.M.: Went to sleep.

1:30 A.M.: Woke up. Had more late-night pie.

2:00 A.M.: Back to sleep. I dreamed that I drove an eighteen-wheeler into the crash pit with fireworks coming out of the exhaust. Sweet!

PROOF PEOPLE LOVE ME

Muscle Man's pecs are gross, but oddly hypnotic.

I'd be miserable without you, bro. You're my best friend.

This guy is better at mentoring than anyone I've ever seen.

My Mitch is the best boyfriend. He's so romantic and he has the best sense of humor!

THE MANY LOOKS OF MUSCLE MAN

Most of the time, you'll see Muscle Man in his favorite blue shirt and black pants—but he looks good in just about anything.

Fancy Muscle Man:
Hey, bros, I looked
so awesome!
Buff Muscle Man:
Savage!
Ninja Muscle Man:
For costume parties,
or kung fu fighting.

Holiday Muscle Man: Because you've got to rock out Hanukkah in style.
Genius Muscle Man: What to wear after a brain-scrambling machine turns you into a physics professor.
Presidential Muscle Man: Just call me Honest Mitch.

Pirate Muscle Man: Aaaargh, bro!
Bowling Muscle Man: I'm looking good on the lanes.
Business Casual Muscle Man: I wore this to celebrate Benson's work anniversary.

WHAT'S ON MUSCLE MAN'S MIND?

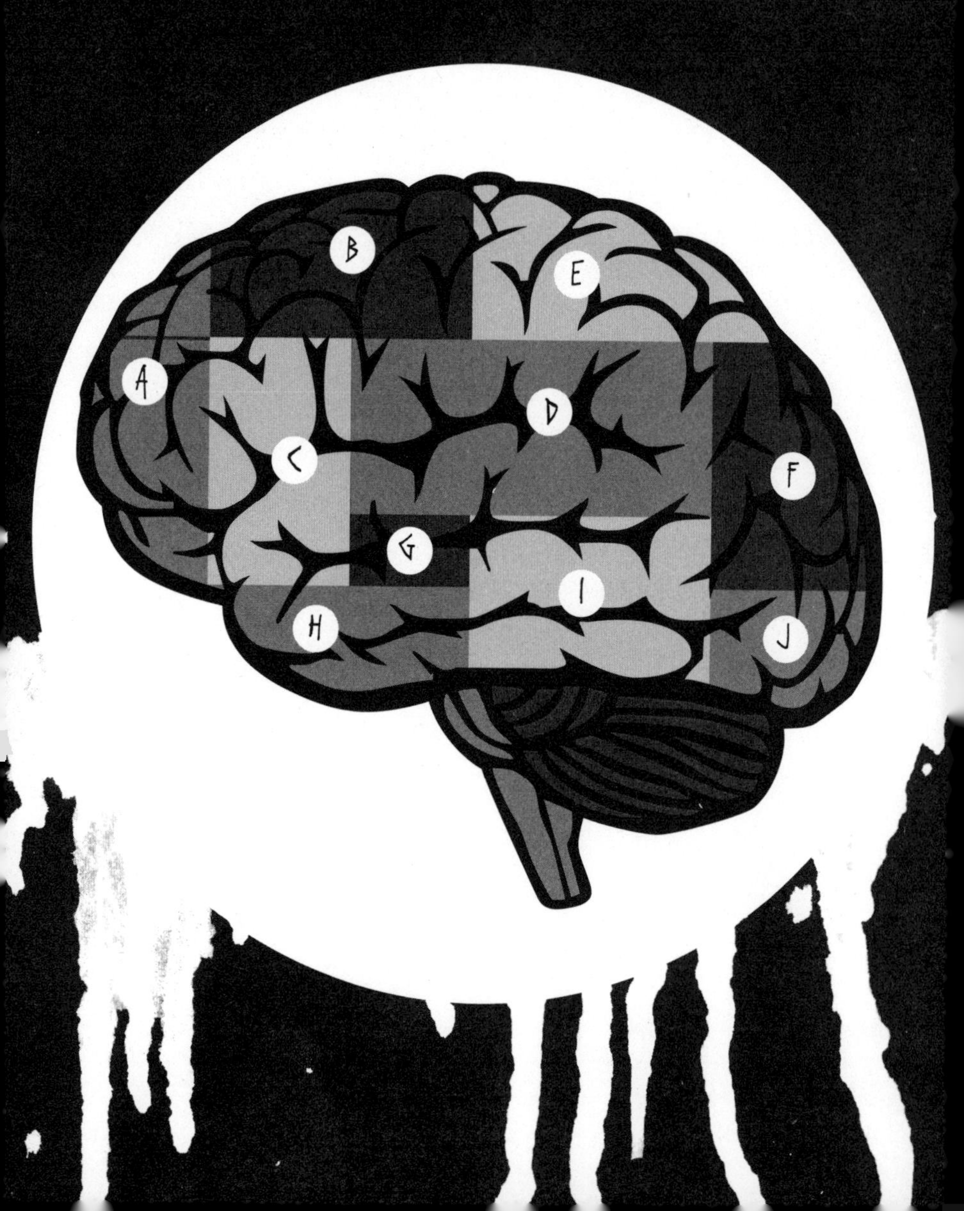

You may think I am a pretty simple guy, but this diagram shows just how deep I really am.

A. MY MOM

B. SWEET FIGHTING MOVES

C. PLANNING NEXT PRANK

D. WHAT'S FOR LUNCH?

E. LYRICS TO '80S HEAVY METAL SONGS

F. I KNOW A GUY WHO . . .

G. GOOD TIMES WITH HFG

H. SECRETS TO AWESOMENESS

I. STARLA

J. MEMORIES OF MUSCLE DAD

So you're probably wondering, "How did you get so awesome at doing air drum solos, Muscle Man?" Well, it took years of practice listening to awesome drum solos by my favorite band, Fist Pump.

I also learned a lot from Benson! Hair to the Throne is my favorite band ever. They totally got me through high school. The drum solo on their first album is the most epic drum solo in history. It features 150 pieces of percussion. And I never knew it, but Benson performed the solo before he got kicked out of the band! Nobody believed Benson, but he proved it to us by playing the solo at the Park. It was legendary, bro!
Some guy in Denmark tried it, and his skeleton caught on fire!

WELCOME TO MY PALACE
This trailer is the third best thing that's ever happened to me. I won it in a hot-dog-eating contest.
PIZZA
Pizza box: You never know when you might need
Sofa: For watching TV, playing video games, sleeping, and cuddling with Starla.

Sunroof
Breakfast nook
Piles of Clothes:
I never have to
search my closet for
something to wear.
Planter:
It used to be a
bowl of chili;
now it's more of
a houseplant.

THE QUOTABLE MUSCLE MAN

Part of being as awesome as I am is knowing how to talk. Although, you might not want to say some of these things out loud without actual muscle power to back you up.

"Can't you toolboxes see I'm busy organizing my toolboxes?"

"Coffee is for people who don't have adrenaline!"

"I don't train losers to lose. I train winners to win!"

"Nobody calls me Mitch except my girlfriend. And the guy who checks my license at the airport."

"I'm saying what's on my mind, bro. I'm just real like that."

"Who here knows more about the ladies? Me, or Single McSingleton?"

"It was hard, but we didn't give up. That's what makes us guys."

"I can't work. I'm busy stuffing my facehole."

"Is there something on my face? Then quit staring, bro!"

"It's not over till I say it's over, ladies!"

"Shut your wormhole. I'm listening to my jams."

"Get out of the way, jerkface. We need to use your time machine!"

"Sometimes you gotta sacrifice for the ones you love."

"I'm gonna turn your face into a meatball pizza!"

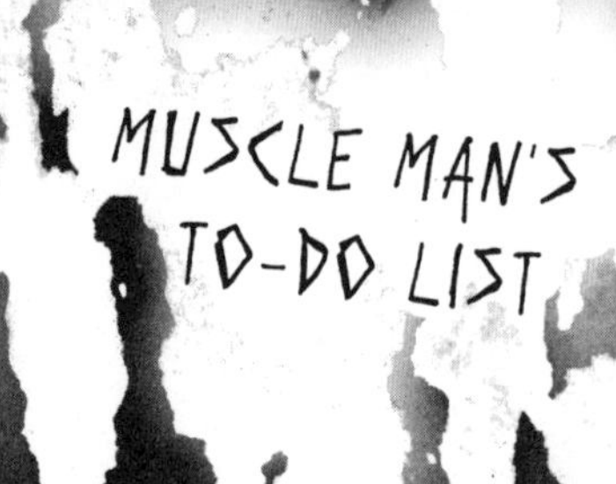

To Do:

1. Prank Mordecai and Rigby
2. ~~Mow lawn outside trailer~~
3. Make Thomas mow lawn outside trailer
4. Go to Starla's curling match
5. ~~Wash golf cart~~
6. Make Thomas wash golf cart
7. Hang with Fives
8. Rock out to my jams
9. Prank Mordecai and Rigby again
10. Invent a new flavor of soda

Yeah, I think this internship's gonna be really cool.

You know who else has a to-do list? My mom!

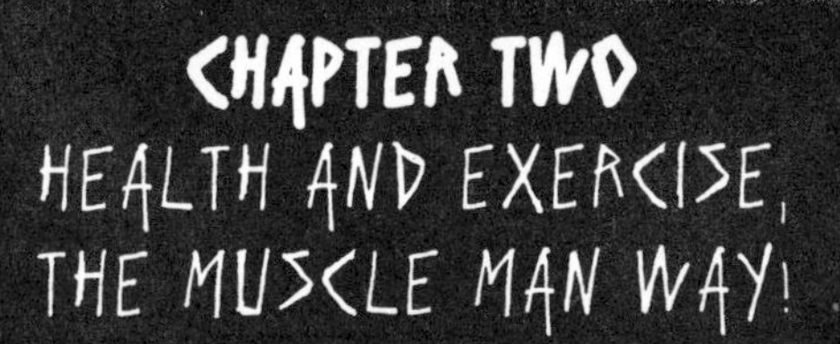

CHAPTER TWO
HEALTH AND EXERCISE, THE MUSCLE MAN WAY!

Do bullies on the beach kick sand in your face? Do your friends call you "wimp"? Nobody disrespects me like that, and you know why? Because I'm Muscle Man! So if you want to know the secrets to how I maintain my sweet physique and awesome stamina, check out my tips in this chapter.

Health tips from Muscle Man? Seriously? No way, dude!

MEET MUSCLE MAN

The only things I've got going for me are my flowing mane and rippling muscles.

A. Seventies shag haircut—the next best thing to a mullet

B. Bloodshot eyes due to lack of sleep

C. Skin the color of moldy cheese

D. Several teeth missing, but that doesn't hurt his killer smile

E. All right, ladies, stains happen

F. Looks wobbly, but capable of crushing a watermelon

G. Calloused hand from constantly high-fiving Hi-Five Ghost

H. Once got third-degree burns on 70 percent of his butt from the seat warmers on the Smärten Kärten golf cart

If Muscle Man's belly gets any bigger, we'll have to add it to the payroll!

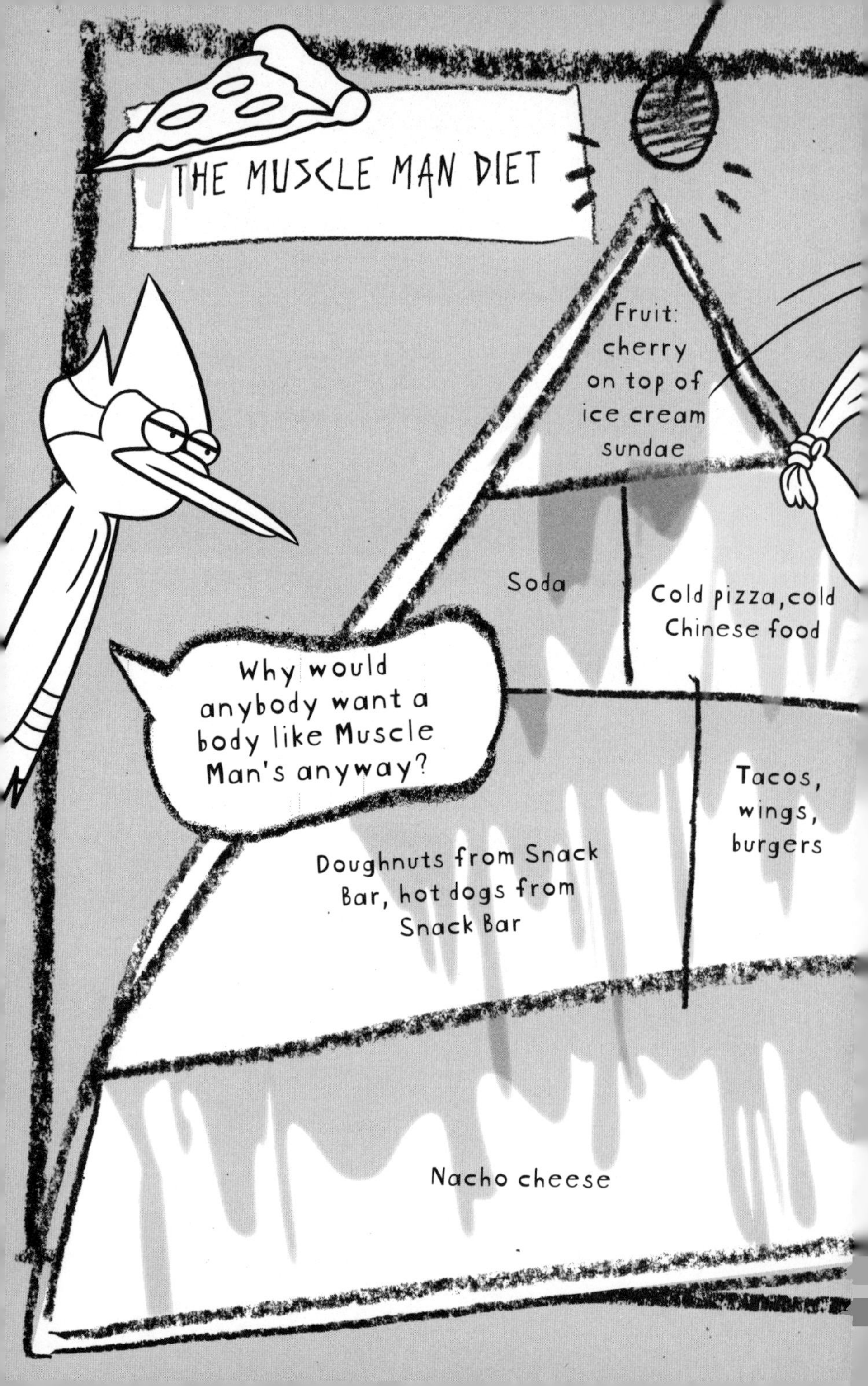
THE MUSCLE MAN DIET
Fruit:
cherry
on top of
ice cream
sundae
Soda
Cold pizza, cold
Chinese food
Why would
anybody want a
body like Muscle
Man's anyway?
Tacos,
wings,
burgers
Doughnuts from Snack
Bar, hot dogs from
Snack Bar
Nacho cheese

You can't get a rocking bod like mine without following a strict diet. And I'm not talking about crummy salad and yogurt. Eat the way I do every day, and soon you'll have a body just like mine.
AND ALWAYS FOLLOW These Tips:
1.Three meals a day is for chumps. Don't forget brunch, pre-dinner, late-night snack, and second breakfast.
2.The person who consumes the most calories wins.
3.If you have to eat vegetables, fry them.
4.Don't worry if you eat so much that you puke. That means there's room for more!

There's a reason everyone calls me Muscle Man. I'm a bodybuilding champion. When I was younger, Muscle Dad gave me a workout video. I had it all—muscles, technique, the total package. I won the Bicep-tennial bodybuilding cup. Then I kinda got bored with it all.

EXHIBIT A:

Years later, this jerk Dale from the gym was hassling m friends and me, so I entered the Bicep-tennial again. I might have lost some muscle mass, but I proved that I could still win with technique. So I performed . . . **THE SHREDDER**. I know this is a guidebook, but I can't explain this one to you. It's too dangerous, bro!

EXHIBIT B:

If done correctly, this move will shred the competition. If not done correctly, it will shred all your muscles, causing instant death!

HOW TO SMELL LIKE MUSCLE MAN

Hey, it's Mordecai. I can't keep my trap shut anymore—I just have to butt in. I mean, why would anyone ***want*** to smell like Muscle Man? No offense, he's my friend and everything, but the dude seriously reeks. But if for some crazy reason you actually do want to smell like Muscle Man, here's what you need to do:

1. Always use your pants to wipe the cheese sauce off your hands when you eat nachos.
2. Never wash your clothes. If you do, wash them in the toilet.
3. Keep a hard-boiled egg in your pocket. Never take it out.
4. Store your shoes in a litter box.
5. Take a shower—once every six months.
6. Never open the windows of your trailer.
7. Run for five miles, and then sleep in your sweaty clothes. (Oh, wait—Muscle Man would never run for five miles.)
8. Roll around in barf.

If you follow every one of these steps, you'll smell almost as bad as Muscle Man—almost.

STENCH AS A WEAPON
In the Night Owl's Standoff for the Steel contest, Muscle Man uses his stinky sweat to eliminate three of the contestants.
Sorry, dude, but you smell like barf!
YOU smell like barf!
Stop telling each other that.
Muscle Man releases noxious fumes all the time!

FUN THINGS TO DO WITH AWESOME MAN PECS

1. They're perfect for hypnotizing the ladies.
2. Use them to warm up some hot dogs.
3. Go dancing: They add an extra shimmy to your shake.
4. Their gentle sway can put babies to sleep.
5. Baby ducks love to cuddle with them.
6. Can be used as weapons in the event of a smackdown.
7. Carry stuff with them—it's like having two extra hands.
8. Make extra money as a bikini model.
9. Play them like bongos.
10. Did I mention hypnotizing the ladies?

Once I developed my awesome pecs, other dudes got in on the act.
The sensei from Death Kwon Do: using man pecs as a weapon.
CITY COMMUNITY COLLEGE
The Guardians of Eternal Youth: letting man pecs rule for all eternity.

WORKOUT SLANG

If you're going to spend time in the gym, you've got to talk like a pro.

BULKING UP:
adding muscle mass

BURPEE:
a squat thrust that ends with a vertical jump

CORE:
the abdominal and back muscles in the trunk of your body

GUN SHOW:
muscular arms

Who wants tickets to the gun show?

PECS:
short for pectorals—muscles in a man's chest

Ladies love my sweet man pecs.

GYM RAT:
someone who works out morning, noon, and night

HAMMIES:
hamstrings—muscles on the back of the thigh

NEWBIE:
someone new to the gym

Rigby is such a newbie. He couldn't even do one pull-up!

REP:
one complete movement of one exercise

RIPPED:
having good muscle definition

I told you I was ripped!

SKULLCRUSHER:
a lifting move that brings the dumbbell within inches of your forehead.

"WHAT'S YOUR MAX?":
How much can you lift?

CHAPTER THREE
FOOD

It takes a lot of food to feed an awesome body like mine—A LOT. But I don't shove just anything in my gullet. I have turned eating into an art form, bro. And you can, too.

MUSCLE BELLY
My belly is legendary—it's smooth, round, green, and hangs over my belt. How did I create such a magnificent stomach? Take a look inside and see.
C.
B.
A.
D.
E.
J.
G.
F.
H.
I.

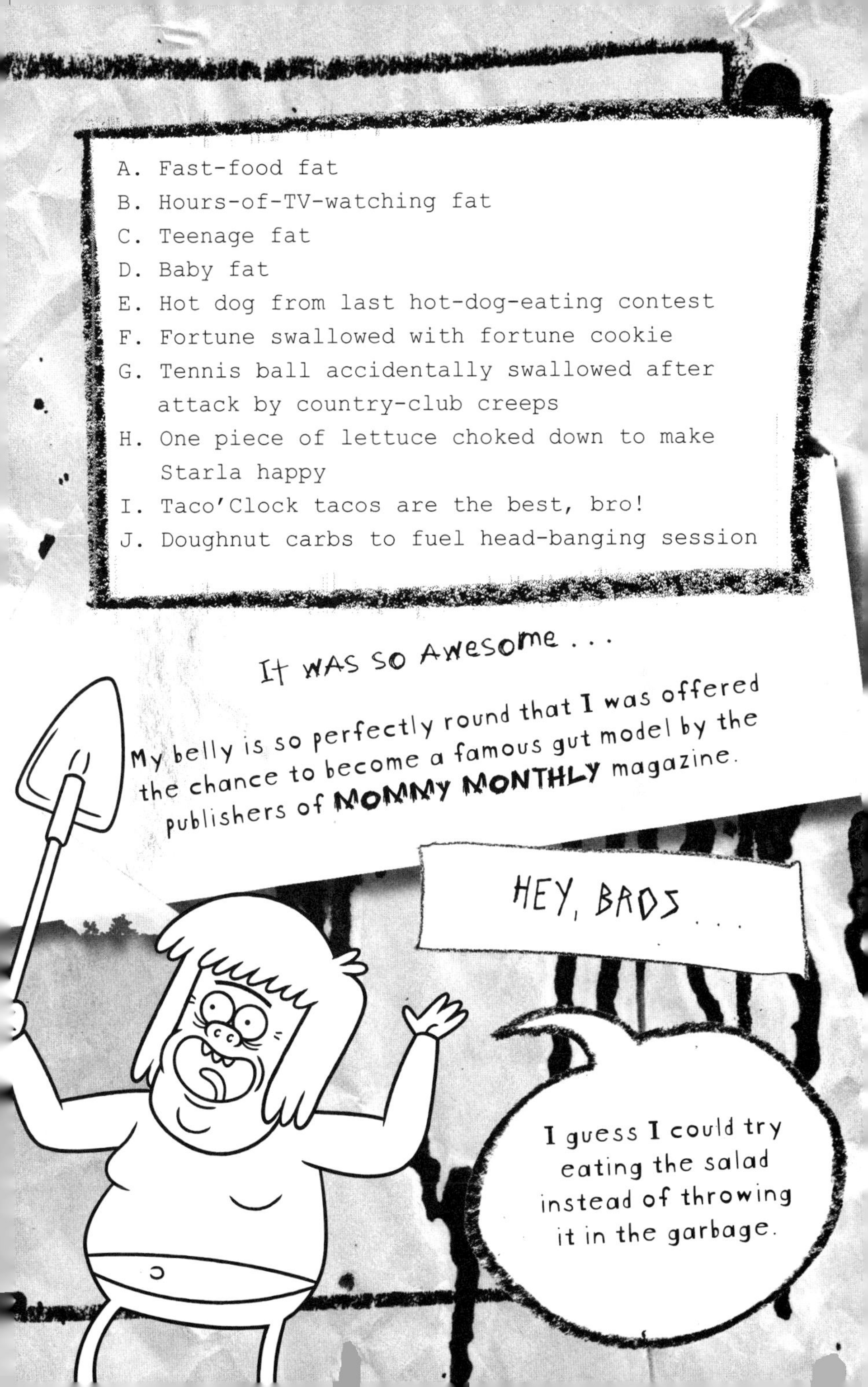
A. Fast-food fat
B. Hours-of-TV-watching fat
C. Teenage fat
D. Baby fat
E. Hot dog from last hot-dog-eating contest
F. Fortune swallowed with fortune cookie
G. Tennis ball accidentally swallowed after attack by country-club creeps
H. One piece of lettuce choked down to make Starla happy
I. Taco'Clock tacos are the best, bro!
J. Doughnut carbs to fuel head-banging session
It WAS SO AWesome . . .
My belly is so perfectly round that I was offered the chance to become a famous gut model by the publishers of MOMMY MONTHLY magazine.
HEY, BROS . . .
I guess I could try eating the salad instead of throwing it in the garbage.

HOW TO WIN A HOT-DOG-EATING CONTEST

Winning hot-dog-eating contests is one of my major skills, bros. Why do **I** do it? Well, for one thing it's a great way to impress the ladies. You can also win sweet prizes. That's how **I** won my trailer, and that place is like a palace inside. And even if you lose, you still get to eat a bunch of free hot dogs, which is pretty cool. **I** never had to train to become a professional hot-dog eater. **I** was born that way, bros. But you're probably going to need some tips.

1. Stretch your belly: You might think you have to starve yourself before the contest. Wrong! The day before, eat some stuff and drink water to help expand your stomach to make room for the hot dogs that are coming.
2. Wet it: Using water to mush your food is totally legit! It's how Japan wins all the time.
3. Exercise: The experts say you're supposed to exercise so eating contests won't make you fat. You can do that if you want to, but I'm happy with my sweet physique already.
4. Don't hurl: Even when you're at your limit and feel like you're gonna puke your guts out, never give up!

Hot-dog-eating-contest competitor Frank Jones was so angry that he lost to Muscle Man, he posed as a health inspector so he could take Muscle Man's trailer.

It WAS SO AWESOME . . .

CHEATING DEATH

Death told me I would die during a hot-dog-eating contest. To save my soul, I challenged Death. At first, it looked like I was doomed. Death choked down a mountain of hot dogs super fast, and I couldn't keep up. Then Starla showed up to support her man, and she and I started making out. That was too much for Death. He puked, and I won the contest—and saved my soul.

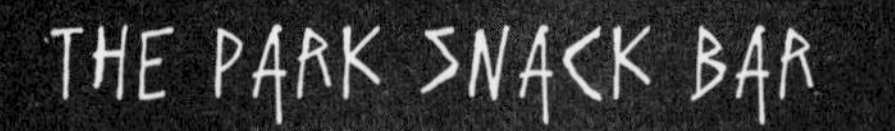

THE PARK SNACK BAR

Hi-Five Ghost and I work at the Snack Bar a lot. It can be boring sometimes, but mostly it's pretty cool because it's got all the major food groups there: sugar, grease, salt, and nacho cheese sauce. Everything's tasty, but Fives and I came up with some secret combos that are pretty sweet.

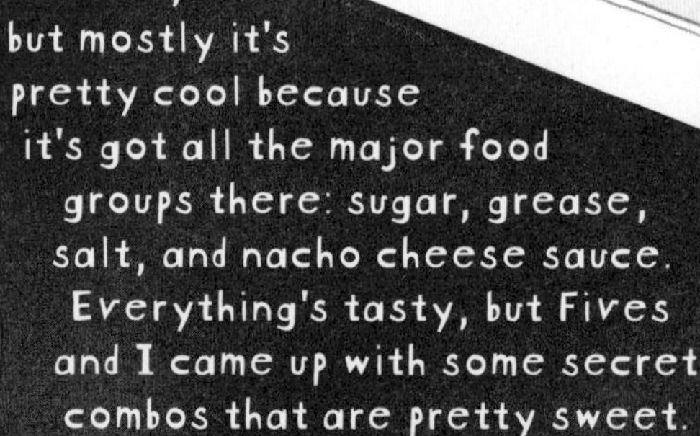

DOUGHNUTS + DEEP FRYER: You can pretty much put anything in the deep fryer, but deep-fried doughnuts totally rock.

POPCORN + CUPCAKE: Who needs wimpy sprinkles when you can put popcorn on top of your cupcake?

HOT DOG + ICE CREAM SANDWICH: Instead of a bun, squish your hot dog between the layers of an ice cream sandwich. It's like eating dinner and dessert at the same time.

NACHO CHEESE SAUCE + CANDY BAR: Trust me, cheese sauce makes everything better.

Consuming too much food at the Snack Bar can be dangerous to your health. Just ask Rigby. After gorging on junk food his body deserted him.

REGULAR PLACES TO EAT

The Snack Bar might be awesome, but if you're visiting the Park, there are plenty of places to eat. Check out my reviews before you chow down.

JIMBRO'S BURRITOS

Their Every Meat Burrito is made of bison, crustacean, naked mole rat . . . and every other meat. Sounds awesome, but it mostly tastes like chicken.

BISTRO EN LA PARC

This place blows. Only go here if you're a snooty snootbag who acts like a jerk.

CANDY'S DONUTS

Just don't order the double-glazed apple fritters, or you might end up in an alternate dimension.

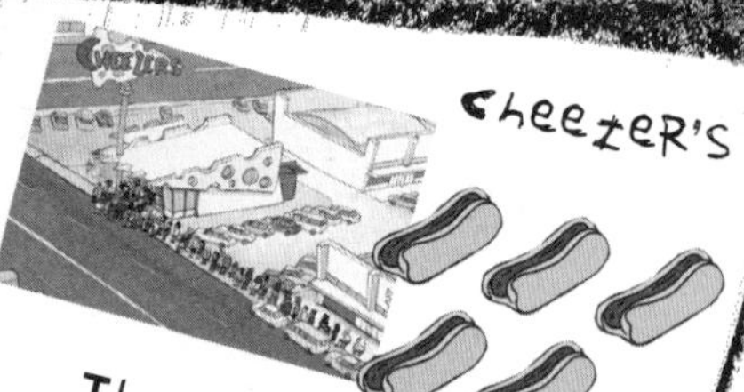

CHEEZER'S

They make the best grilled-cheese sandwiches ever. Astronauts like to hang out there. They must like grilled cheese.

DEATH KWON DO PIZZA AND SUBS

DEATH KWON DO PIZZA AND SUBS

The pizza is decent, but the subs are to die for—literally. Their most popular menu item is the Death Sandwich. If you don't eat it wearing cut-off shorts and a mullet, you'll die.

Fry It Up

They fry everything here. You can get fried chicken, fried hot dogs, fried salad, fried milk, fried wings, fried muffin tops, and the mother of all fried things—a cream-cheese doughnut stuffed with fried chicken.

Hot Buns Doggery

The best doggery in town. My guy Marty works there, and I defeated Death in a hot-dog-eating contest here, so it's got an awesome vibe.

South of the Line

Their spicy chili rellenos are really spicy. They're made with gunpowder, though, so they're no fun on the back end, if you know what I mean.

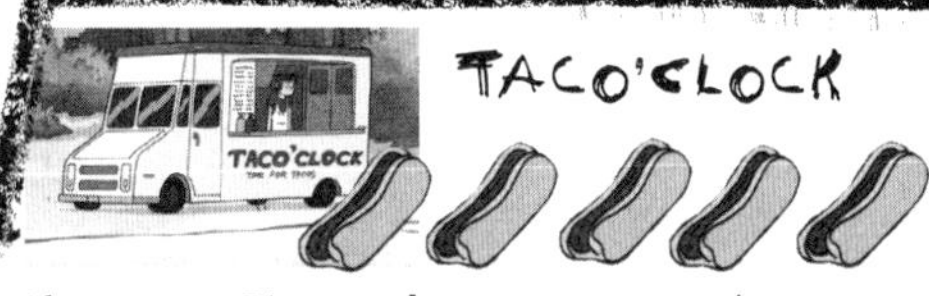

TACO'CLOCK

My guy Jimmy's taco truck moves around a lot, but it's worth looking for. He sells tacos around the clock, so if you're craving beef and cheese at four in the morning, Jimmy will hook you up.

Steak Me Amadeus

This is another fancy rip-off place for snooty snootbags, but if you get ahold of some free Amadeus Dollars, the steak is pretty good.

Wing Kingdom

They have all kinds of wings: Asian wings, buffalo wings, ranch wings, or my favorite—Asian buffalo ranch wings. Plus it's got a romantic atmosphere perfect for impressing the ladies. Starla and I come here all the time.

Sometimes, you just need a piece of meat cooked on a grill and stuck between two buns. I keep a meat locker outside my trailer so that I can make a tasty burger any time I want. But if I want to be chilling instead of grilling, I grab a burger from the Grill 'Em Up food truck.

The Ulti-Meatum!

What's the best burger in the world? Definitely the Ulti-Meatum from Grill 'Em Up. It's a cheeseburger stuffed inside a cheeseburger with two deep-fried cheeseburgers as buns, and special ketchup from the Himalayas. It's so amazing, it's only offered every hundred years. Like the saying says, "Anyone who doesn't eat one is a chump!"

Burger Facts

- Americans eat about thirteen billion hamburgers a year. That's enough to circle the earth thirty-two times.
- Hamburgers get their name from a kind of steak from Hamburg, Germany.
- The first fast-food restaurant sold hamburgers for five cents each.
- The biggest hamburger in the world was sold by a restaurant in Pennsylvania in 2007. It weighed 123 pounds.
- In 2010, Takeru Kobayashi set the world record for eating the most hamburgers in three minutes: ten. They had pickles on them.

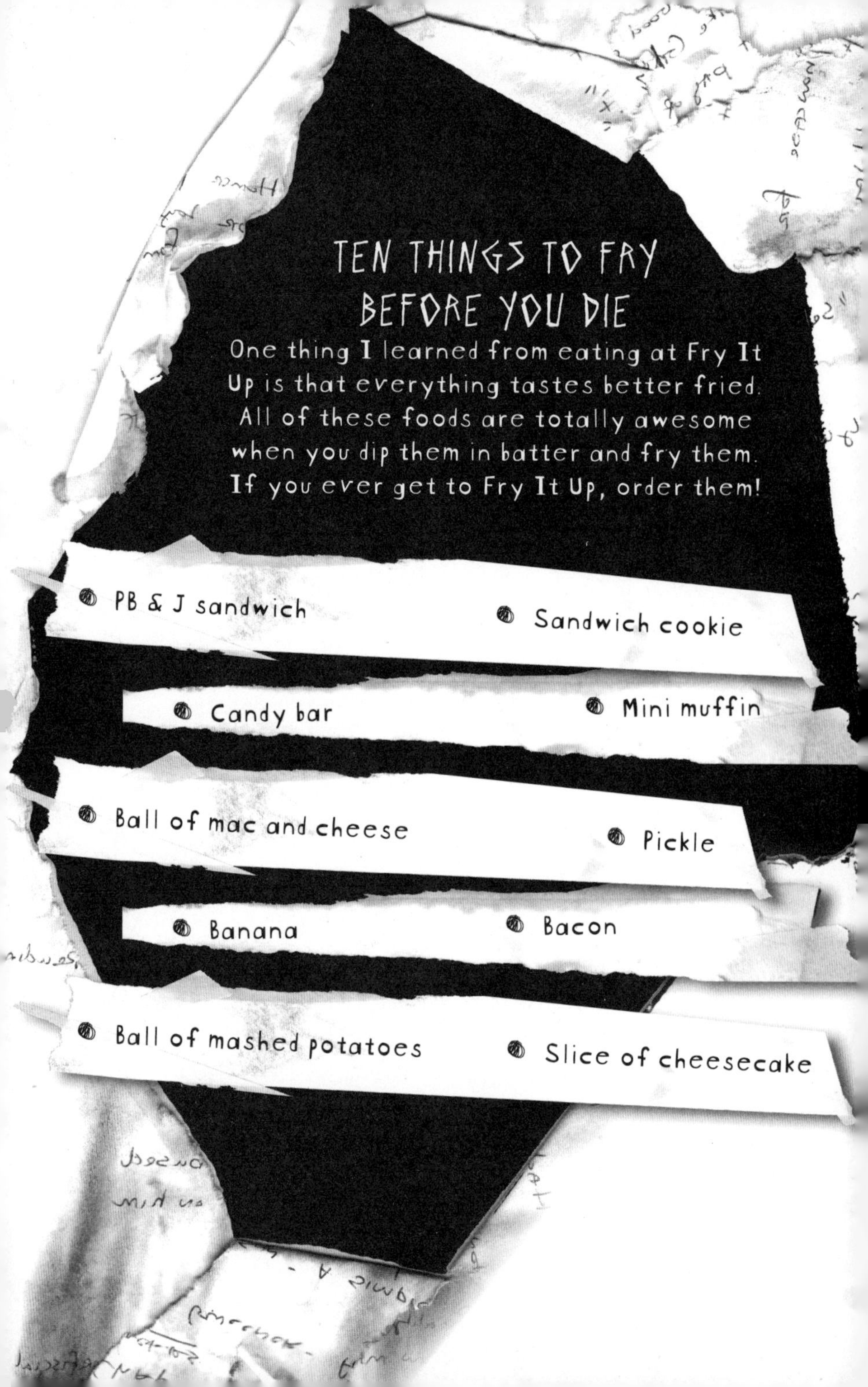
TEN THINGS TO FRY BEFORE YOU DIE
One thing I learned from eating at Fry It Up is that everything tastes better fried. All of these foods are totally awesome when you dip them in batter and fry them. If you ever get to Fry It Up, order them!
PB & J sandwich
Sandwich cookie
Candy bar
Mini muffin
Ball of mac and cheese
Pickle
Banana
Bacon
Ball of mashed potatoes
Slice of cheesecake

CHAPTER FOUR
ON THE JOB
Working in the Park is a sweet job. There's fresh air, plenty of places to disappear for a while, and I get to hang out with my best bro, Fives, all day. But pretty much any job can be sweet if you take my advice.
SODA

HOW TO AVOID WORK

One of the reasons I love my job is that I have figured out how to get my work done at my own pace—without making Benson angry, like Mordecai and Rigby always do. Trust me, it's an art form. Check out how I turned a boring chore into an awesome day:

START

The Park. Benson asks you to pick up a lemon tree from the nursery.

Pick up lemon tree from nursery.

Prank your friends.

END

Return to the Park with the lemon tree. Benson congratulates you on a great job.

Stop for lunch at the Taco'Clock truck. Check in with Benson so he doesn't worry.

"Go for it! I know you guys will get it done."

Wire the golf cart to make it go crazy fast.

Take the souped-up golf cart off the road. Woo-hoo!

Get stopped by police officer. He admires your awesome driving skills.

Head to the arcade to play *Giganto-Fist*.

Go to the movie theater to check out a 3-D matinee.

Go bowling. Hi-Five Ghost bowls a strike!

DEALING WITH PEOPLE

TYPE: THE DESTROYER

Good points: This type is always offering to fix things.

Bad points: That's because they always break them in the first place. Everything they touch ends up in flames. Or outer space.

How to deal: The only way to control a Destroyer is to strap him to your chest so he doesn't leave your sight.

Need more coffee . . .

Type: The SLACKER

Good points: This type doesn't cause as many problems as a Destroyer.

Bad points: Slackers will try to avoid work but aren't smart enough to do it without getting caught by the boss.

How to deal: If you want a Slacker to do some work, call him a Slacker. He'll try to prove you wrong.

Type: The Fixer

Good points: When you've got a problem, a Fixer knows all the answers and never complains about fixing them.

Bad points: Being around somebody who knows all the answers can make you lazy.

How to deal: Give a Fixer a hand once in a while. You might learn something.

Type: The Gentleman

Good points: Always polite and positive, a Gentleman makes everyone around him want to act a little nicer.

Bad points: He is a little spacey.

How to deal: Look out for a Gentleman and make sure no one takes advantage of him.

Type: The Angry Boss

Good points: When he's in a good mood, he'll reward his employees.

Bad points: He's almost never in a good mood.

How to deal: Don't argue with him when he gives you a job you don't want—and then go take a nap. You'll get to it eventually, and he'll never know the difference.

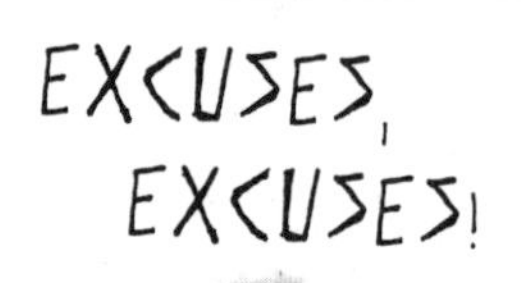

My mom told me not to.

They were giving out free cake.

Sometimes, you just don't feel like working. No sweat. Just use one of these sweet excuses. They'll get you out of anything!

Death captured my soul and stuck it in a bottle, and I couldn't get out.

I ate too many hot dogs and got sick.

It was destroyed by a flock of wild geese.

I was being chased by a herd of unicorns.
My fortune cookie told me not to.
I had to do a solid for my best friend.
I spun around too much and got dizzy.
My golf cart got a flat tire.
It was stolen by the gnome that lives in a cave under my house.
An evil guy erased my brain with a machine, and I forgot who I was.

ULTIMATE GOLF CART

Sometimes when Fives and I are riding around on the golf cart, I like to think about how I would trick out my ultimate golf cart. I think it would look something like this:

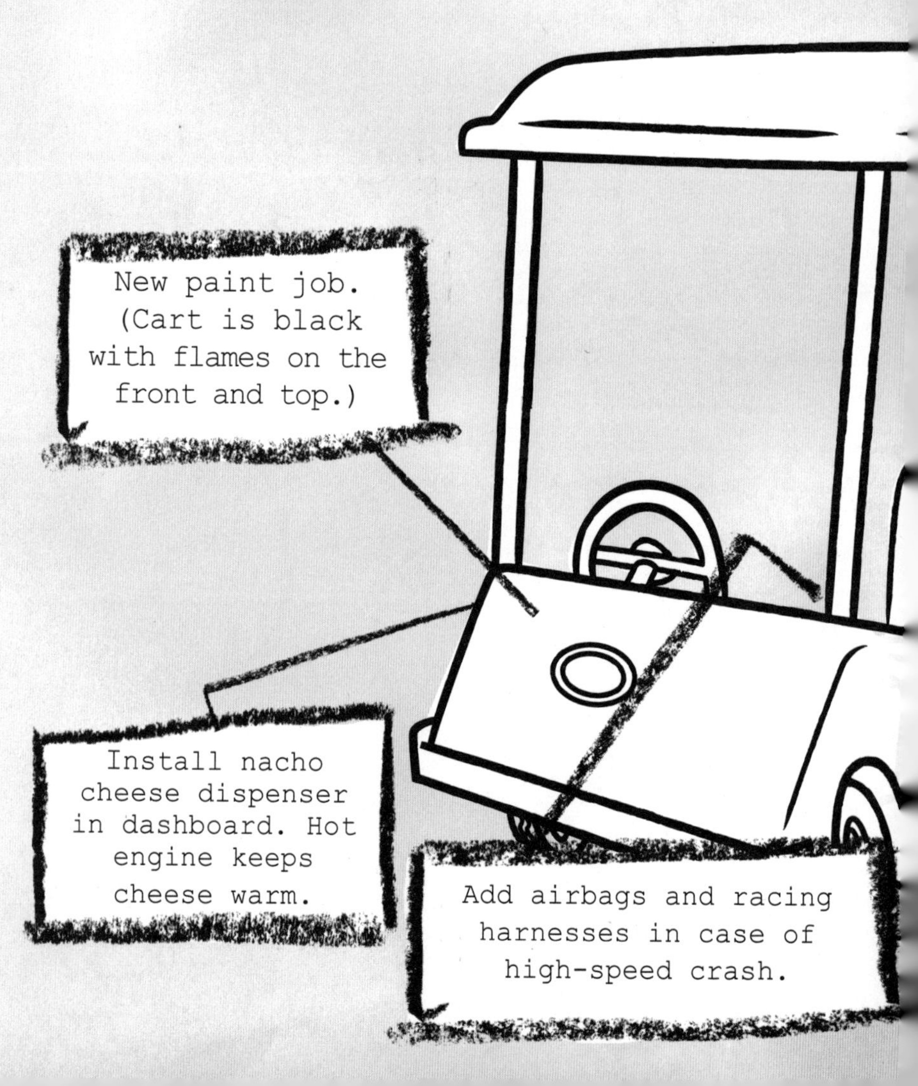

Whale-tail spoiler to keep the back end down when we're flying across the Park.
Replace the backseat with two subwoofers for a sweet sound system.
Replace the puny gas engine with a massive turbo engine.
Add a nitrous bottle for boosts of extra speed.
Trick out the skirt with neon lights to light up the grass underneath.

MUSCLE MAN'S DREAM JOBS

I love my job at the Park, but there are some other jobs I think I'd be great at:

- Stand-up comic
- Roadie for Fist Pump
- Professional speed-eating competitor
- Race-car driver
- Stuntman
- Professional photographer
- Video-game tester
- Host of a viral-video TV show
- Drummer in a heavy metal band
- Deejay
- Model

That's right. I dabble in photography.

Good evening, everyone! So, I just threw out my old couch. It weighed about three hundred pounds and smelled like a pile of butts. You know who else smells like a pile of butts? My mom!

CHAPTER FIVE
RELATIONSHIPS, AKA "THE LADIES"

I don't mean to brag, but I have always had a smooth way with the ladies. Most of it comes to me naturally. Babes get hypnotized by my flowing mane and ripped muscles. These days, though, there's only room in my heart for one, so I'll give you some tips for how to get the attention of the special lady.

No other lady compares to my Starla. She's fun, she's beautiful, and she's foxy when she breaks things. Plus, she completes my life. My lady's love gives me all the strength I need.

MEET STARLA!

Name:	Starla Gutsmandottir
Also known as:	Muscle Woman
Works at:	Icy Hot Jewelry Apparel
Likes:	Romantic movies, romantic gestures, romantic restaurants
Dislikes:	Anyone who messes with her man
Quote:	"Stop the car, Mom. My man needs me!"

It WAS SO AWESOME . . .

When Starla gets a new boyfriend, she tattoos his name on her lower back. So far, the names are Muscle Man, Steve, Muscle Man, Mordecai, and Muscle Man. (Mordecai dated her and dumped her in an attempt to get her back together with Muscle Man.)

No one gets me like you do, babe!

THE DATING GUIDE

1. TRY NEW STUFF: Mordecai and Rigby didn't want the Tants that Pops gave them, but Starla and I swung by for a sweet pizza dinner.

2. SHOW YOUR FEELINGS: This one's kinda hard, but if you do show your feelings you won't be able to keep the ladies away. Trust me.

If you want to keep your lady happy, you've got to take her on great dates. Stick to my dating tips and you can't go wrong.

You're the light of my life. The fire that burns in my heart. The one. Starla—will you be my Muscle Woman?

3. MAKE THE MOMENT: At the end of the date, make sure you get your good-night kiss. Like so:

Me: Did you have fun tonight, babe?
Starla: I always do.
Me: I hope you saved room for dessert.
Starla: I always do.

Then pucker up!

4. KISS IN PUBLIC: Some people are uptight about public displays of affection. I say, if you love your lady,

5. STAND UP FOR YOUR LADY: Once you and your lady are tight, make sure she knows you've got her back.

"If Starla's rhubarb pie doesn't win, the next pie you taste will be in a tube, because you'll be in a hospital, hooked up to life support."

BEING FANCY

Fancy restaurants are lame. But sometimes you gotta take your lady to one to impress her. Mordecai and Rigby did me a solid and helped me get fancy for a dinner with Starla and her parents. If you ever have to go to a fancy restaurant, do what I did:

STEP 1: LOOK THE PART

Most fancy restaurants make you wear a dumb suit. I got mine at the Awkward and Oblong store.

STEP 2: GREET YOUR GUESTS WITH A FIRM HANDSHAKE.

Just make sure you don't have potato chip crumbs on your hand, first.

STEP 3: OPEN THE DOO FOR YOUR GUESTS.

STEP 4: SEAT YOUR GUESTS.

When you get to your fancy table, pull out a chair for each guest so they can sit down. This is a perfect opportunity for a prank, but resist the urge to pull the chair out from underneath them, even though that would be hilarious.

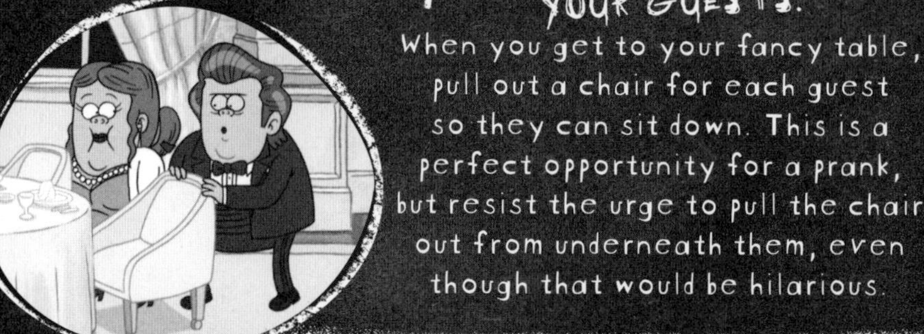

STEP 5: BRING UP FANCY CONVERSATION TOPICS.

Some good ones are: the weather, your job, your guest's job, fancy sports like golf and polo.

STEP 6: MIND YOUR MANNERS.

Practice good manners at the table. Put your fancy napkin on your lap. Chew with your mouth closed. Luckily, fancy restaurants don't have straws, so you won't be tempted to stick them up your nose and pretend to be a walrus.

When Fancy Waiters Get Wild

If you follow the steps above, your fancy dinner should go just fine. But if your snooty waiter tries to throw you out of the restaurant, then forget about being fancy and defend yourself:

- If a waiter charges you, hit him under the chin with an uppercut.
- If your waiter has a saber, use a food tray as a shield.
- Waiter too much to handle? Grab a friend, hold hands, and mow him down.
- If a waiter comes at you with a salad fork, trip him!

MUSCLE MEN
DON'T CRY
Muscle Man, are you taking a shower so we can't see you crying?
No, it's just the sound of water hitting the drain.

Crying is for ladies! I don't cry . . . well, most of the time I don't. But when Starla broke up with me, it broke my heart. I couldn't help myself, and I bawled like a little baby. If you ever find yourself in that situation, and you don't want to look weak in front your lady, then use one of these excuses:

I'm not crying . . .
. . . my eyes are peeing.
. . . it's raining.
. . . I got muscle-building powder in my eye.
. . . it's workout sweat.
. . . my taco was extra spicy.
. . . I'm allergic to your perfume.
. . . my awesomeness is leaking out.
. . . my brain is dripping.
. . . I drank too much water.
. . . there were extra onions on my burger, babe.
. . . I just got out of the shower.
. . . I was in a staring contest.
. . . I'm lubricating my eyes.

Hey, sorry to interrupt again, but I just want to point out that the Muscle Man way of kissing is totally gross. Every time I see it I want to barf. So if you want to make people barf, then go ahead and kiss like Muscle Man.

- Make disgusting slurping noises.
- Close your eyes so tight, it hurts.
- Grunt a lot.
- Make out in inappropriate places, like the middle of a roller rink.
- Don't care if anyone's watching you.

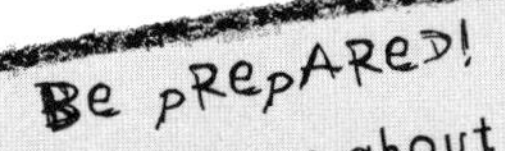

If you're serious about kissing someone, then you need to be prepared. I carry all the essentials: mints, gum, mint strips, breath spray, mouthwash, toothpaste and floss. Make sure you don't use them all at once, though, or your breath might transform into a deadly freeze that encases you and everyone around you in ice. Long story.

As much as I want to vomit right now, those two were made for each other.

HOW TO COVER UP A BAD HAIRCUT

My guy Tony is a great barber, but sometimes even the best mess up. Once he shaved a bald spot on the top of my head, and I didn't want Starla to see. If you ever get a bad haircut, just try one of these methods to cover it up while it grows back.

1. PARTY TIME: Cover up your bad hair with a sombrero. If people ask, just tell them that party time is anytime! Woo-hoo!

2. THE COMBOVER: This works if you get a chunk taken out of your hair. Just take the hair you do have and comb it over the bald spot. Classic.

3. NOT-SO-BALD SPRAY: Another solution if you've got hair missing. Kind of like covering up the chipped paint on your car.

4. CREATE A DISTRACTION: If your hair is gross, then accentuate another part of your body that's awesome, so people don't notice your bad hair. I hypnotized Starla with my sweet man pecs.

5. WIG OUT: I guess if you can get your hands on a wig, that's always a good option. But there's always the danger that you might end up looking worse than you did before.

6. CAP IT: A trucker cap not only covers up a bad haircut, but also the netting in the back can keep your head cool when you're rocking out.

7. HIDE: When all else fails, just don't leave your house until your hair grows back!

SAY IT IN SONG

If you really want to impress the girl you're dating, why not write a song? I did, and I even got it played on the radio (right before defeating an evil computer program and blowing up a radio station). But your adventures in songwriting don't have to be so complicated. Today marks the anniversary of a special day in my relationship with Starla. It's the anniversary of when we first made out. And I want it to be really special for Starla.

WRITE YOUR OWN . . .

Fill in the blanks to create the perfect song for that special someone in your life.

Hey, ______ (name of girlfriend), this song is for you.
I really like your ______ (eyes/smile/hair), and everything you do.
You're really awesome, ______ (name of girlfriend),
You're everything to me.
I like when we eat ______ (favorite food),
And watch ______ (favorite TV show) on TV.
Hey, ______ (name of girlfriend), you're always in my heart.
Let's eat some ______ (bean/beef/chicken) burritos, and
ride in my golf cart.

"STARLA"

by Muscle Man

I used to be a loser, hangin' out with my loser friends,
And the first time we made out, it made my neck hair stand on end.
Oh Starla, Starla-uh-uh!
I guess it's like my heart is spinning doughnuts.
You're the cheese upon my burger, I'm the mustard on your bun.
Just like the perfect burger, our love's never overdone.
You're the ice cube in my cola,
I'm the ketchup on your fries.
And I'll punch the face of any bro,
Who says so otherwise!
Oh Starla!
But I knew you'd be my lady,
And I'm your Muscle Man.

GETTING OVER A BAD BREAKUP

Starla's broken up with me twice, and I hope she never breaks up with me again. But if she does, I'll know what to do, and you can do the same if your lady ever dumps you:

1. Stuff your face: Food makes everything better. I once ate a whole container of Muscle Maker 3000 powder to fill the hole that Starla left in my heart.
2. Take a mental-health day from work: Some other guys will have to do your work while you get over your broken heart.
3. Get back out there: Grocery stores are a great place to meet women. Check out a lady's cart to see if she's single. American cheese singles and single servings of soup are a good clue that she might be lookin' for love.
4. Listen to your favorite song: over and over and over again.
5. Hang out with your bros: Ladies may break your heart, but your bros will always be there for you.
6. If all else fails, get her back: Because it ain't over until it's over. Or until she takes out a restraining order on you.

CHAPTER SIX
PRANKS

Everything I know about pranking, I learned from my old man. Nobody compares to him. He was the master. You might not become as good a prankster as my dad, but if you read this chapter you'll learn how to prank with the best.

Being pranked by Muscle Man all the time is the **worst!**

The one thing that a Sorrenstein almost never screws up is a prank. Before you start pranking, you need two things: tools and rules.

Tools

If you keep this stuff on hand, you'll always be seconds away from a prank.

1. Whoopee cushion. A classic. What's funnier than an instant fart?
2. Fake (or real) spiders and snakes. Always good for a scream.
3. Chewing gum. Chew it up, put it in the path of a jogger, and watch the fun.
4. Kick-me sign. Tape it to your unsuspecting victim's back and you're good to go.
5. Balloons. Water balloons are an essential weapon in any prank war.

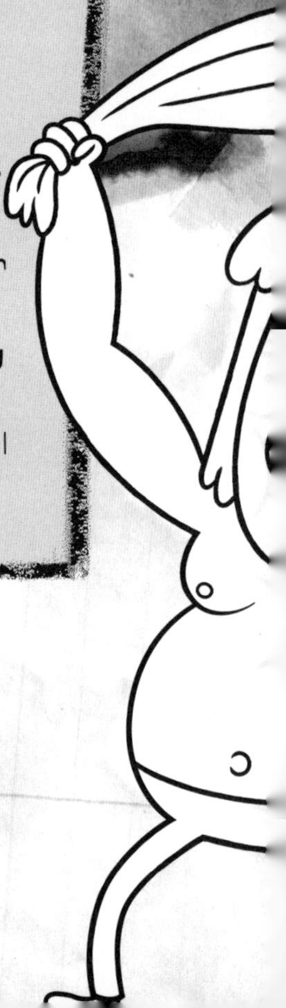

RULES

Yeah, even pranks have rules.

1. Pranks should never hurt anybody. That's not cool, bro.
2. If somebody pranks you first, it's okay to prank them back. In fact, it's mandatory.
3. Don't tell anyone about the prank you're planning, unless you trust them and need help. They might feel bad for whoever's being pranked and spoil everything.
4. Your prank shouldn't destroy anybody's property.
5. Pranks should always be about having fun!

PRANKS AROUND THE HOUSE

Once you've got your rules and tools, you're ready to start pranking. You can probably pull off one of these pranks today.

1. **SINK PRANK:** You know the sprayer on the sink that you use to spray down dishes? Take a rubber band and wrap it around the sprayer and the handle so that the handle is pressed down. Then walk away. The next person to use the sink will get sprayed in the face!

2. **SODA SURPRISE:** This one's a classic. Right before mealtime, shake up your victim's soda can while he or she isn't looking. When your victim pops the top—splash!

3. **I CAN'T HEAR YOU!:** Put clear tape, like packing tape, over the mouthpiece of your victim's landline phone. When they get or make a call, the person on the other end won't be able to hear them, and they'll end up shouting until they figure out what's wrong.

4. **MOLDY MILK:** At night, put a few drops of green food coloring in a carton of milk. The first person to use it in the morning will get a surprise!

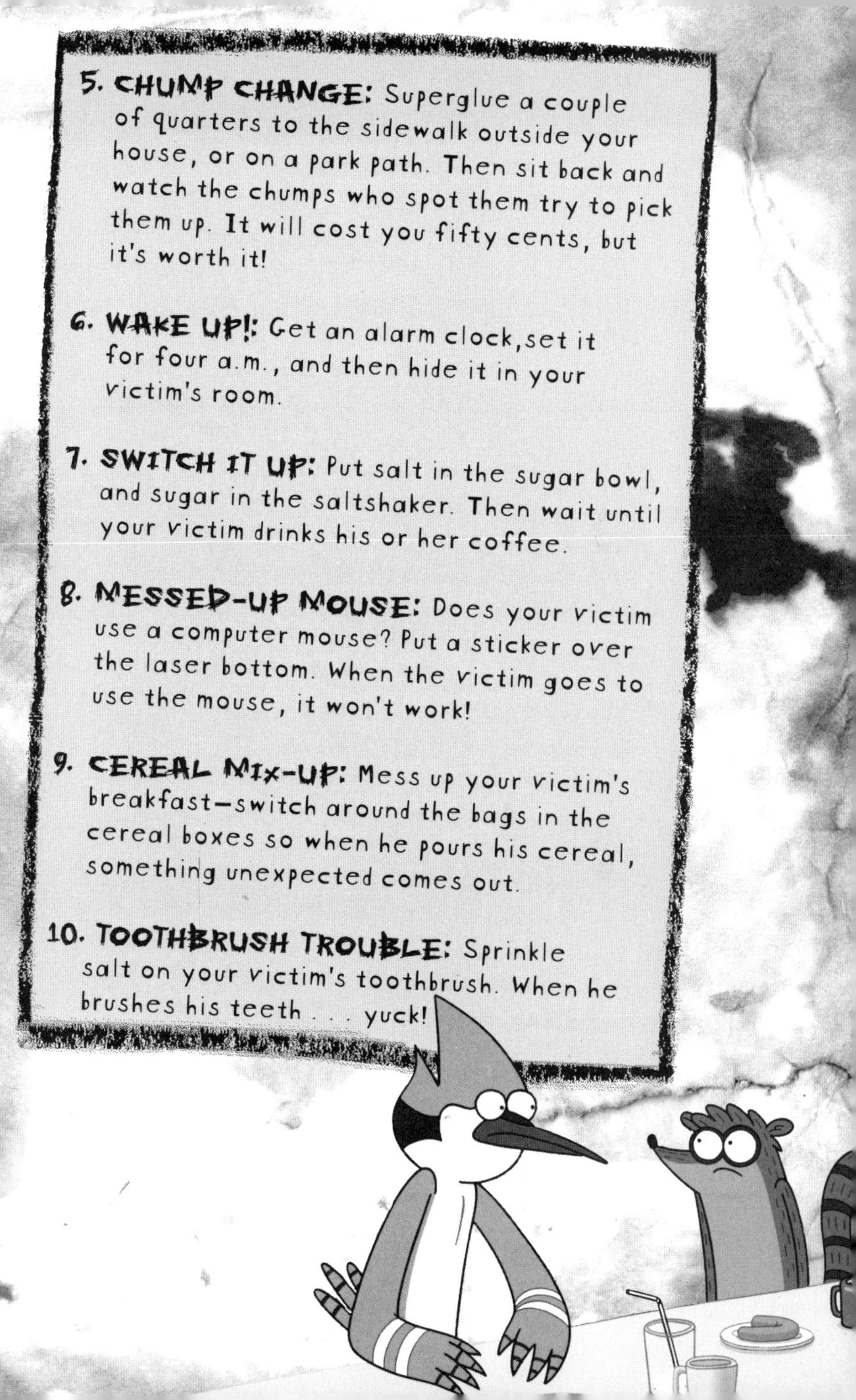

5. **CHUMP CHANGE:** Superglue a couple of quarters to the sidewalk outside your house, or on a park path. Then sit back and watch the chumps who spot them try to pick them up. It will cost you fifty cents, but it's worth it!

6. **WAKE UP!:** Get an alarm clock, set it for four a.m., and then hide it in your victim's room.

7. **SWITCH IT UP:** Put salt in the sugar bowl, and sugar in the saltshaker. Then wait until your victim drinks his or her coffee.

8. **MESSED-UP MOUSE:** Does your victim use a computer mouse? Put a sticker over the laser bottom. When the victim goes to use the mouse, it won't work!

9. **CEREAL MIX-UP:** Mess up your victim's breakfast—switch around the bags in the cereal boxes so when he pours his cereal, something unexpected comes out.

10. **TOOTHBRUSH TROUBLE:** Sprinkle salt on your victim's toothbrush. When he brushes his teeth . . . yuck!

MY GREATEST PRANKS

Simple pranks are awesome, but when you become a master of pranks like me, you need to step up your game. My greatest pranks involved lies, huge special effects, and tons of cash. And they were both aimed at Mordecai and Rigby.

DEATH OF THE PARTY

It all started when Rigby was choking, and Mordecai made him cough up his chokewad. It landed in his soda, and soda splashed in my face. They thought it was funny. I wanted revenge. Here's how I got it:

I invited everybody I knew to a costume birthday party for Hi-Five Ghost. Everybody except Mordecai and Rigby, that is.

I knew those chumps would be desperate to get in. They were. When they couldn't get in the door, they got HFG's brother, Low-Five Ghost, to turn them into ghosts so they could walk through the wall.

I got Fives and his dad to tell Mordecai and Rigby that they would stay as ghosts forever unless they scared somebody. They decided to scare me.

I pretended to have a heart attack and die. You should have seen their faces. Best prank ever!

The PRANK'S on You

This one started during Thomas's first week at the Park. I pranked him good as part of his initiation week. Then I kept pranking Thomas, and Mordecai and Rigby got mad. But that was all part of my plan:

Mordecai and Rigby tried to convince Thomas to prank me back, but Thomas didn't want to. So they played a prank on me and told me that Thomas did it.

I got super mad and flew into a crazy rage. Mordecai and Rigby tried to stop me as I chased down Thomas in his car.

I ripped a shed from the ground and threw it on the car. It looked like I crushed Thomas. Mordecai and Rigby freaked out. But once again, it was all part of the prank.

Thomas was in on it with me! I wasn't mad at him at all. Mordecai and Rigby looked like chumps, and Thomas had turned into a bona fide prankster.

MEET THE PRANKSTERS OF EAST PINES

Name:	Gene
Occupation:	Manager of East Pines Park
Looks like:	A vending machine
Likes:	East Pines Park. He believes it's superior to all other parks.
Dislikes:	All other parks.
Quote:	"Say good-bye to your park, 'cause when we're done with it, there'll be nothing left!"

EAST PINES PARK WORKERS

These guys look more like soldiers than park workers. In the end, though, they should have stuck to mowing lawns and cleaning restaurants. Nobody can out-prank Muscle Man!

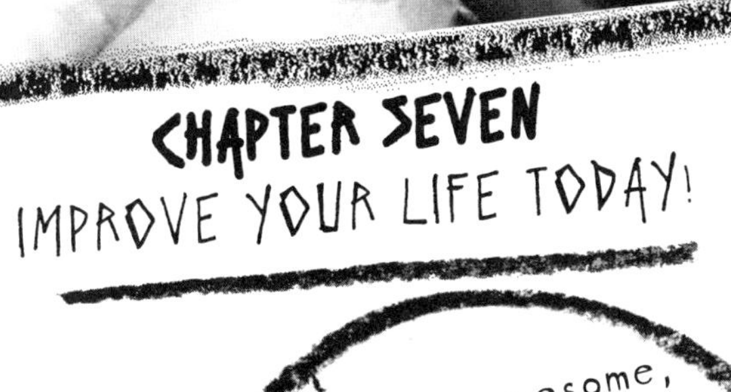

CHAPTER SEVEN

IMPROVE YOUR LIFE TODAY!

If you want to be truly awesome, you've got to live life, bro. Don't let fear stop you. Fear is for chumps. Some things on this list I've done already—and some are on my list of things to do.

1. Spin doughnuts in a golf cart.
2. Enter a hot-dog-eating contest.
3. Eat one food from each of your favorite restaurants in one day.
4. Throw a surprise party for somebody.
5. Eat an ice cream sandwich. The premium kind.
6. Travel to the future in a time machine.
7. Go skating at a roller rink.
8. See your favorite band in concert.
9. Wrestle a bear and win.
10. Get a tattoo of a wolf on your belly, and make it talk all the time.
11. Use shot-put equipment to fight off a zombie horde.
12. Build a water slide.
13. Win a muscle-building contest.
14. Eat one of every flavor of cheese curls that exists.
15. Learn guitar and write a sick heavy-metal jam.
16. Go on a road trip.
17. Grow your hair really long.
18. Adopt a dog and train it to get sodas out of the fridge for you.
19. Destroy a box of dark magic in a lava pit to save the world for Santa.
20. Become a video-game champion.

THE GOD OF BASKETBALL'S FUNDAMENTALS

1. Warm up before you practice. Stretch your muscles so you'll be limber on the court.

2. Practice taking shots until you think you can't stand it anymore. Then practice some more.

3. Keep your head up when you dribble so you can see what the rest of your teammates are doing.

4. After you pass, keep moving! Be ready to accept another pass when it comes your way.

5. Learn how to rebound. When your opponent is in position to make a basket, turn your back to him or her. Make sure you're about two feet from the rim. Bend your knees so you have a low center of gravity, and keep your hands out in front of you at chest height with your elbows bent. If the ball rebounds, you'll be closer to the rim and can get the ball before your opponent does.

MUSCLE MAN'S GUIDE TO BASKETBALL

1. Taunt your opponent mercilessly. Say "In your face!" every time you score or block a shot.

2. Don't be afraid to sweat. If you don't sweat, you won't win.

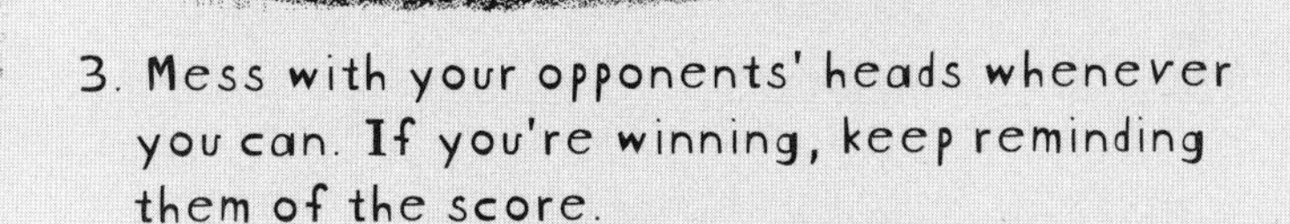

3. Mess with your opponents' heads whenever you can. If you're winning, keep reminding them of the score.

4. Insist on playing by street rules. If you're losing, have your worst player pretend to be injured. Then you can replace him with any player in the Park.

When I get time on the house computer, I usually spend it watching Internet videos. Man, I never get tired of watching Wedgie Ninja do his magic. Here's my list of what I think makes videos go viral:
1. Animals doing human stuff. Like cats playing the piano. Or Road Hog, who tries to jump over a canyon in his car. Hilarious!
2. Farting. Especially animals farting. Like Glocken Bear, only he plays a glockenspiel when he farts on you.
3. Guy does something stupid and gets hurt. Classic! Funny to watch, but not something you want to try at home, bro.
4. Feats of strength. Like the viral video I made where I smash watermelons with my belly.
5. Mad skills. Like when Hi-Fives juggled five basketballs while he was riding a unicycle.
BUT SERIOUSLY KIDS, DON'T TRY THESE AT HOME!!!

MUSCLE MAN'S GUIDE TO WATCHING VIRAL VIDEOS

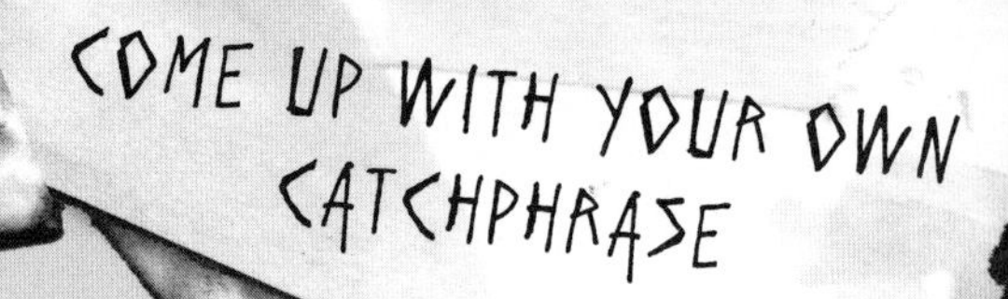

START WITH AN EXCLAMATION . . .

Hey
Smell my
Watch it
Awesome
Always
Never
Please
Whoa
Yeah
Sweet

. . . AND ADD A NOUN . . .

Dude
Kids
Ladies
Babe
Shorts

. . . OR A VERB...

Burn
Surrender
Do It
Check It
Shut It
Give Up

Oh no, bro! You don't have your own catchphrase? Well, you can't use mine. But you can choose some words from these columns to come up with your own.

WRITE YOUR NEW CATCHPHRASE HERE:

____

CHAPTER EIGHT
FRIENDS AND ENEMIES

MEET MUSCLE DAD

Name:	Muscle Dad Sorrenstein
Former occupation:	Forklift operator
Likes:	Playing pranks; telling jokes about his wife
Dislikes:	Mean truckers
Quote:	"Breaker, breaker. Muscle Daddy here. You copy?"

It Happened

When Muscle Man was growing up, Muscle Dad pretended to be a trucker, but he really worked as a forklift operator. Muscle Man found out when he took Mordecai and Rigby to help him spread his dad's ashes at the Trucker Hall of Fame. Some Trucker Ghosts tried to stop them, but the ghost of Muscle Dad appeared, and together, he and Muscle Man fended off the ghosts.

Muscle Man's Brother, John

Even though Muscle Dad wasn't really a trucker, John followed in his footsteps. He drives an eighteen-wheeler and is always there to help Muscle Man when he needs him.

Maybe he wasn't the best trucker in the world . . . or a trucker in the world. But he was my dad.

Pranks Muscle Dad Pulled on Muscle Man:

- Shook up a can of soda so it exploded in his face
- Filled his birthday piñata with scorpions.
- Rigged a bucket of water to fall on Muscle Man and his prom date.

WHEN YOUR BEST FRIEND IS A GHOST

HI-FIVE GHOST

Name:	Hi-Five Ghost
Nicknames:	Fives, HFG
Likes:	High-fiving, Muscle Man's "my mom" jokes
Dislikes:	Funerals
Skills:	Moving through solid objects; hot-wiring cars; making dunk shots; playing the trumpet
Quote:	"I'd be miserable without you, bro. You're my best friend!"

Fives is the perfect best friend. He's great at basketball, he totally gets me, and he loves to play pranks. Plus, he's always there when I need to high-five someone. Awesome!

Hands On

Most of the time, you can only see one of Hi-Five Ghost's hands, but a second hand appears when he plays basketball. In a viral video he used five hands to juggle five basketballs.

It Happened

Once, Muscle Man got depressed when none of his friends would hang out with him—not even Hi-Five Ghost, who had to go to his brother's graduation from the police academy. Muscle Man quit his job to become a gut model, but he didn't really want to do it. When a Grease Monster started attacking everybody at a party to celebrate Muscle Man, Fives saved him by transforming into a huge protective bubble. Muscle Man realized that his friends only wanted what was best for him, and came back to the Park.

Low-Five Ghost

Like Muscle Man, Hi-Five Ghost has a big brother. Low-Five Ghost works as a police officer and has the ability to turn people into ghosts.

GUYS' NIGHT!
What's the best way to hang out with your bros? GUYS' NIGHT! It's when you get together once a month and do guy stuff with your guy friends. Here's how to have an awesome guys' night:
1. Eat junk food. Chips, soda, hoagies, microwave burritos, and cookies are all perfect to eat on Guys' Night.
2. Check out manly magazines, like *Hot Rod* magazine.
3. Eat more junk food. Get a bunch of pizzas delivered.
4. Play a manly card game, like five-card stud.
5. Play manly videos games, like *Dig Champs* or *Broken Bonez*.
6. Watch manly movies, like war movies, kung fu movies, and horror movies.

SODA
SODA
CHIPS

ROAD TRIP!

Going on a road trip is another awesome thing to do with your friends. Follow my tips to have the best road trip ever.

1. Crank some tunes: I like to bang my head to bands like Adrenaline and Fist Pump.

2. Bring snacks: Burgers give me the energy I need for long car trips. If you run out, you can always get beef-jerky sticks at a gas station. They're full of beefy goodness.

3. Take turns driving with your friends: That way you can catch some zzz's and keep the trip going all night.

4. Whatever you do, don't let Mordecai and Rigby borrow your car for a road trip.

Bad idea! When I fell asleep on my road trip with Mordecai and Rigby, they stopped at an arcade and played video games all night.

5. If you stop at a rest stop, stay away from the truckers: They can be mean jerks. They said mean stuff about my dad.

I like to listen to electropop music on car trips. It helps keep me awake.

Don't forget napkins! Lots of napkins!

Everybody knows the only fuel you need for a road trip is COFFEE!

It wasn't our fault!

Yeah, and Muscle Man's dad was a cool guy!

Aw, thanks, Rigby! I'll go on a road trip with you anytime.

I KNOW A GUY . . .

Even though I'm pretty awesome, I don't know how to do **everything**. That's why you've got to know guys who can hook you up with cool stuff. Here are some of the guys I know:

JIMMY, MY TACO GUY: He works at the Taco'Clock truck and makes my tacos just the way I like them—with extra grease and cheese.

JIMMY, MY ELECTRONICS GUY: Jimmy can hook you up with anything from a LaserDisc player to a free TV. Usually he gets fired for doing it, though.

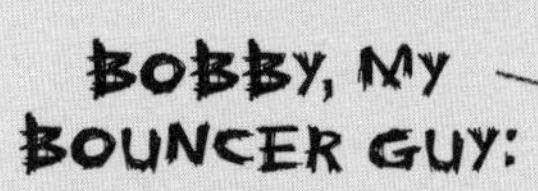

BOBBY, MY BOUNCER GUY: Tired of getting turned away at the coolest clubs? Then you need to get in tight with the bouncer. Bobby's my bro.

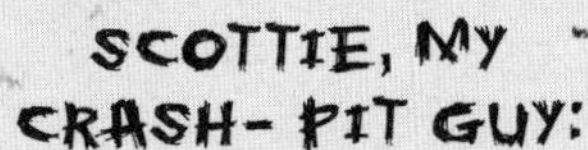

SCOTTIE, MY CRASH-PIT GUY:
Whenever I need a crowd to watch me wreck cars in the crash pit, Scottie's the guy I call. He knows everybody who loves to watch stuff crash.

MARTY, MY HOT-DOG GUY:
Extra onions? Spicy mustard? No problem. Marty from the Hot Buns Doggery always has what I need.

HECTOR, MY FIREWORKS GUY:
Well, he *was* my fireworks guy. He turned out to be an evil cyborg who tried to kill my friends and me. But, man, did he make great fireworks. He sold them out of the back room of the South of the Line Mexican restaurant.

EL DIABLO

Hector kept his greatest firework, El Diablo, in a glass case. A prophecy said that if the firework was lit, it would hunt him down and kill him. Rigby brought El Diablo to the Park, and Hector accidentally set it off. El Diablo turned into a version of the South of the Line logo—a pistol-toting pepper. He took aim at Hector, and the cyborg's days were over.

MEET DEATH

DEATH

Name:	Death
Likes:	Riding his motorcycle, wearing black leather
Dislikes:	The living
Family:	Lives in a manor with his four-armed wife and his demon son, Thomas
Quote:	"I'm in a bit of a rush today, so I'll just go ahead and take Muscle Man's soul."

Yeah, I know Death. When I wiped out on my water slide he came for my soul, but Mordecai and Rigby got it back for me. He wanted my soul again, but I beat him in a hot-dog-eating contest. What a loser!

It HAppened

Muscle Man and his friends first met
Death after Skips killed Rigby during
an arm-wrestling contest. Rigby had
cheated using the PlayCo Armboy, and
when Skips found out, he got angry
and accidentally killed Rigby during an
honest contest. Skips felt so bad that
he made a deal with Death: If he could
beat Death in an arm-wrestling contest,
Death would give Rigby's soul back. If
not, Death could take Skips's soul, too.
In the end, Skips defeated Death—using
a PlayCo Armboy!

The MAGICAL ELements

Did you know that Death is on a bowling team? They call themselves the Magical Elements. The other members are the leader of the Guardians of Eternal Youth; the Wizard; and Gary, the messenger of the Guardians of Eternal Youth.

Magic or not, we're still gonna beat you chumps.

MUSCLE MAN'S MONSTERS

Monsters attack the park employees all the time. Here are a few that Muscle Man has tangled with.

The Huggstables

Little kids might love these cute critters, but they gave me night terrors that caused me to sleepwalk and beat up my friends. Skips ended up using the magic of dream catchers to free them from my dreams.

The Wizard

On Halloween, this wizard got mad that Rigby threw eggs at his house and turned Rigby into a house to get revenge. We tried to fight him off, but he skinned me alive.

Grease Monster

At a party to celebrate becoming a gut model, I decided I didn't want to become a gut model for life. In a fit of rage, I threw random stuff into a deep fryer, bringing the Grease Monster to life. Hi-Five Ghost saved me in the end.

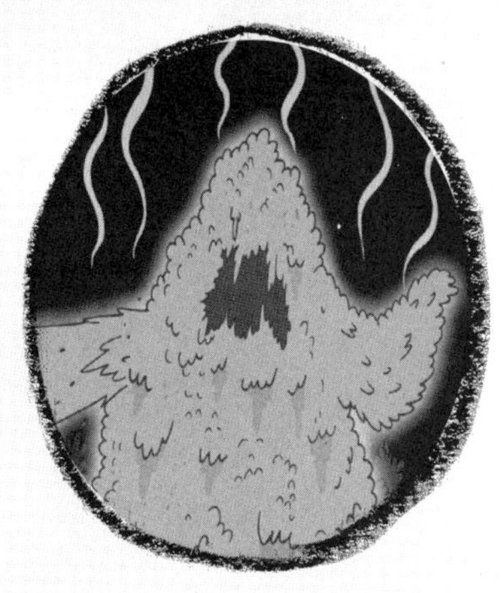

Zombies

I was the only one smart enough to bring sports equipment to the outdoor movie showing in the graveyard. When the dead started coming to life, I started shot-putting their heads off.

Jan the Wallpaper Man

When Mordecai and Rigby hired Jan to wallpaper the house for free so they wouldn't have to do it themselves, they didn't realize they were doing business with a giant spider. I ended up getting eaten by the spider, but in the end Jan was destroyed by some grenades that I had ordered.

Peeps

Benson hired this giant floating eyeball to watch over his park's employees, and it really creeped everyone out. Mordecai got rid of the eyeball by defeating it in a staring contest.

The Night Owl

Started out as a human deejay who held a radio contest to see who could win a vintage Dodge Charger. When Mordecai, Rigby, Fives, and I conspired to end the contest quickly, he froze us in nitrogen to keep his contest going forever. When we thawed out thousands of years later, the Night Owl was half human, half robot. We defeated the Night Owl and used a time machine to turn things back to normal.

Skull Punch

The ghosts of this British heavy-metal band trapped me in their tour RV and tried to destroy me in the crash pit. I escaped, but I had to face them again when a portal between worlds opened up.

I really love my mom. She's the best. People love it when I make jokes that end with "my mom!" You know who else loves jokes that end with "my mom"? My mom!
CHAPTER NINE
MY MOM!

BEST OF MY MOM

I am famous for cracking people up with my "my mom" jokes. You know who else cracks up? My mom! Anyway, here are some of my greatest "my mom" moments.

Well, well, well. Looks like someone needs some supervision. You know who else needs supervision?
My mom!

This songs rocks. You know who else rocks this hard?
My mom!

Jimmy from Taco'Clock: I feel sorry for you guys.
Muscle Man: You know who I feel sorry for? My mom!

Rigby: I guess Muscle Man is only really insulting himself.
Muscle Man: You know who taught Hi-Five to hot-wire the car to get away with slacking off at work and not get in trouble with his boss? My Uncle John. He's a mechanic.
Rigby: That's cool.
Muscle Man: You know who taught him? My mom!

Bobby here lifts like a champ. Hey, Bobby, you know who else lifts like a champ? My mom!

Benson: The options for this month's game night are checkers, cards, Double Dutch, tiddlywinks, and . . . "My mom" isn't a game, Muscle Man. It doesn't even make sense.
Muscle Man: Looks like I win!

Starla: Oh, Mitch! I've never heard you talk about your feelings before.
Muscle Man: You know who else doesn't like to talk about feelings? My mom!

Muscle Man: It's lunchtime. This place has the best tacos in the city. You know who else has the best tacos in the city?
Rigby: Dude, Benson will blow a fuse if he finds out we were slacking off.
Muscle Man: You know who else will blow a fuse if she finds out we were slacking off?
Mordecai: We don't have time for this!
Muscle Man: You know who else doesn't have time for this?
Mordecai and Rigby: Aah!
Muscle Man: You know who else says "Aah!"? My mom!

Boom shaka-laka! Computer rights for a week! You know who else likes to score so she can get computer rights for a week? My mom!

(A children's party clown throws up in his own mouth.) Muscle Man: You know who likes special entertainment like that? My mom!

Health Inspector: You have two paths. Down one, you hand over your trailer and we leave peacefully. The other leads to violence and horror. Muscle Man: You know who else leads to violence and horror? My mom!

Benson: Muscle Man, have you seen Pops today?
Muscle Man: Yeah, and you know who else has seen Pops today?
Benson: Who, your mom?
Muscle Man: I wasn't going to say that. Why does everybody always think I'm going to say, "My mom"?

Guy: These look great, Mitch!
Muscle Man: You know who else looks pregnant in photographs?
My mom!

Benson: Does anyone know who can help us?
Muscle Man: I know someone who can help.
Benson: If you say "my mom," you're fired.
Muscle Man: My mom!
Benson: Get out!
Muscle Man: It was worth it.

(After Pops eats a bunch of doughnuts intended for the staff meeting):
You know who else likes to stuff themselves with the boss's free doughnuts?
My mom!

That joke doesn't make sense. When you say stuff like that, it shouldn't be, "My mom." It should be, "*Your* mom."

No one makes fun of my mom!

These cookies are great. You know who else makes great cookies?
My mom!

SO LONG, BRO!

So that's all there is, bro! If you follow my advice you'll become a totally awesome guy like me. Well, maybe not as awesome as me, but pretty awesome.

Where you gonna go now, Muscle Man?

I don't know. Probably go wherever the wind takes me, I guess. Probably find a place to settle down. And get a burger with a side of onion rings.

THE END

Yeah! Now that's how you write a book, babies!